This book belongs to:

There's
No Place
Like Home

Disney's Out & About With Pooh
A Grow and Learn Library

Published by Advance Publishers
© 1996 Disney Enterprises, Inc.
Based on the Pooh stories by A. A. Milne © The Pooh Properties Trust.
All rights reserved. Printed in the United States.
No part of this book may be reproduced or copied in any form
without written permission from the copyright owner.

Written by Ronald Kidd
Illustrated by Arkadia Illustration Ltd.
Designed by Vickey Bolling
Produced by Bumpy Slide Books

ISBN:1-885222-61-0
10 9 8 7

There was no doubt about it. Wherever Kanga went, Roo went, too. Every day since he was a little baby, Roo had ridden in Kanga's warm, snuggly pouch as she hopped through the forest. It was a nice way to travel, especially if you wanted to nap along the way.

But Roo thought he was too big for that now. He wanted to go places on his own, not just where his mama took him.

As Roo sat under a tree thinking of where he might want to go, a small brown speck came spinning by. Right behind it was Rabbit, who looked as if he might have been chasing the speck for some time.

"Hello, Rabbit," said Roo. "Why are you chasing that speck?"

"It's not a speck," gasped Rabbit, stopping to catch his breath. "It's a maple seed."

Soon Rabbit caught up with the seed and captured it in his cupped hands. Then he showed it to Roo.

"Why was it flying through the air?" Roo asked. "I thought seeds live in the ground."

"They do," said Rabbit. "But sometimes they take a little trip first."

Since Roo was thinking about taking a little trip of his own, he wanted to know more.

"Come on, Roo," said Rabbit. "I'll show you my seed collection."

When they got to Rabbit's garden, Rabbit brought out the big old wooden box where he kept his collection.

"Do all seeds fly when they take a trip?" Roo wanted to know.

"Nope. But these do," explained Rabbit, taking out a white, fuzzy dandelion. "Go ahead, Roo, blow on it!"

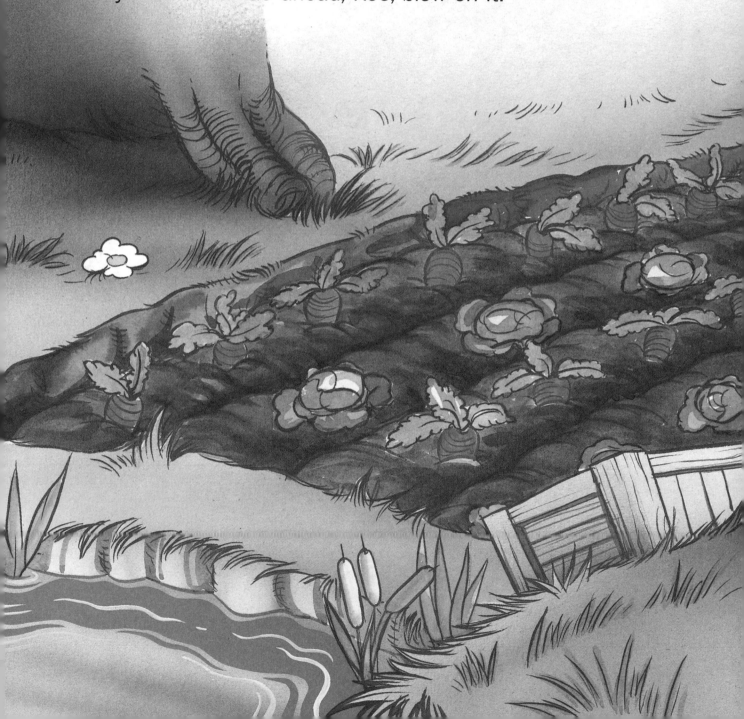

Roo puffed out his cheeks and took a deep breath.
When he blew on the dandelion, the tiny seeds floated off.

Next Rabbit took out a great big coconut.

"That can't be a seed!" exclaimed Roo. "It's too big!"

"But it *is* a seed," said Rabbit. "And instead of flying, this seed floats when it wants to travel."

Rabbit led Roo over to the brook. As Roo watched closely, Rabbit carefully placed the coconut in the water. It spun slowly for a moment, then floated off downstream.

"What else do you have in that box?" Roo asked, poking his head inside.

"I have a seed that doesn't fly or float," Rabbit replied. "It rides!"

Rabbit took out a cocklebur and placed it on the ground near some acorns.

"Now watch," he whispered to Roo.

Soon a squirrel came by, and, sure enough, the cocklebur stuck to its fur.

"Bye-bye, seed!" waved Roo as the squirrel and seed disappeared into the woods.

"Rabbit, why do seeds take trips?" Roo wanted to know. "Seeds need to find the right place to grow, especially one where there's lots of room," Rabbit explained. "So they just fly, float, or ride until they find it."

Roo wanted to travel on his own more than ever — after all, didn't he need room to grow, too?

"Thank you for showing me your collection, Rabbit!" Roo called as he hopped toward Pooh's house.

Pooh was just finishing off a jar of honey when Roo came bounding through the door.

"Pooh," Roo said breathlessly, "have you ever noticed the way dandelion seeds travel?"

But Pooh, being a bear of very little brain, had not.

"Never mind," said Roo. "What I was really wondering was whether you and I could fly your balloon."

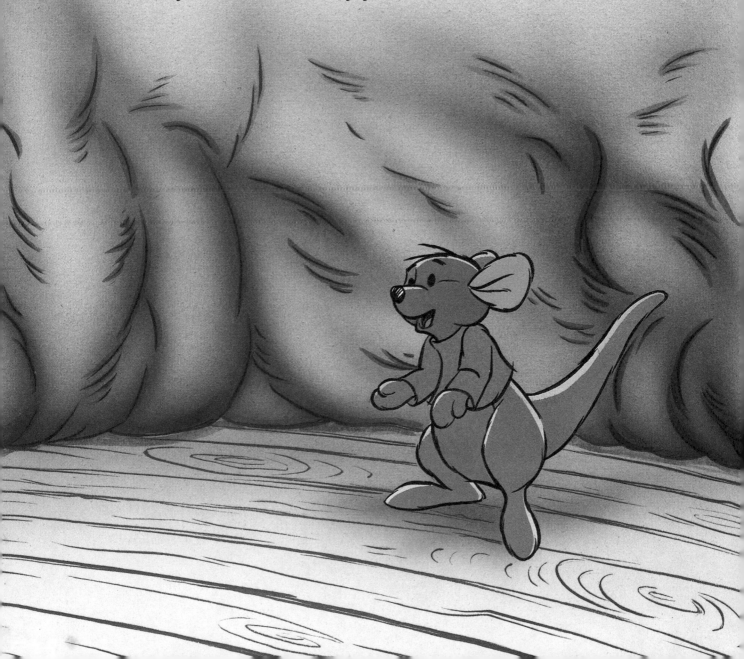

"What a good idea!" said Pooh.

And so, while Roo waited impatiently, Pooh blew up the balloon.

"All set!" Pooh announced as he took hold of the string.

"Yippee!" cried Roo, and he grabbed onto Pooh. Slowly, ever so slowly, they began to rise into the air.

"I'm flying!" shouted Roo.
"Just like a dandelion seed!"
"If you don't mind, Roo,"
Pooh said, "I prefer to think of
us as a little black rain cloud."

Whatever they were, they went floating up to a beehive.
"Time for a little smackerel of something," said Pooh,
reaching into the hive. His paw came out dripping with honey.
Smiling, he said, "I always did like balloons."

Just then a bee buzzed above them, and there was a loud POP!

A moment later the two friends were back on the ground. Next to them was the balloon the buzzing bee had burst.

Pooh, licking his paw, didn't mind a bit, but Roo was disappointed. He got to his feet. "Thank you for helping, Pooh," he said, "but maybe flying isn't the best way for me to travel."

Next Roo went to visit Piglet.

"Piglet," Roo said earnestly, "did you know that some seeds float?"

"Was I supposed to know that?" Piglet asked worriedly.

"No," said Roo. "But do you remember the day it rained and rained, and you had to leave your house in an upside-down umbrella?"

"Yes," Piglet said, brightening. "I remember that."

"Well, if you still have the umbrella, I'd like to use it," said Roo.

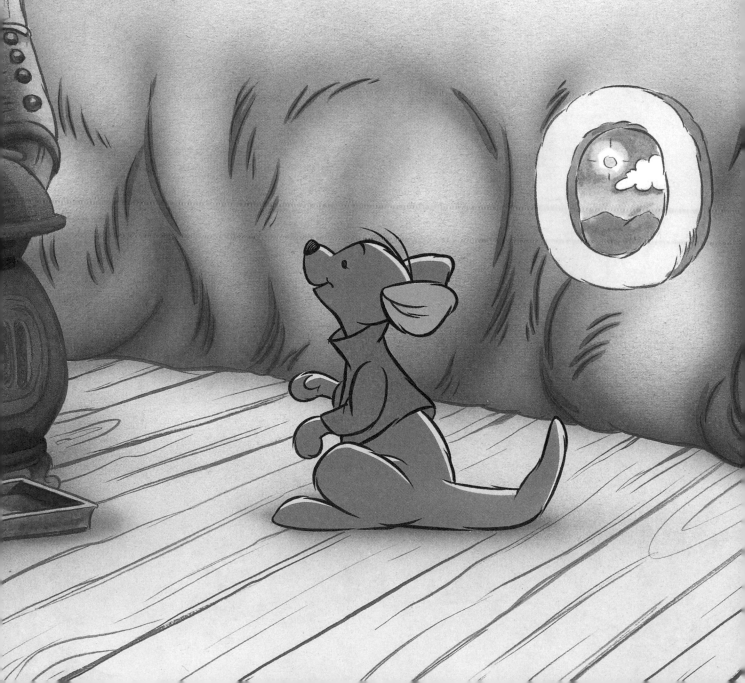

Piglet, who always liked to be helpful, found the umbrella and gave it to Roo. There was some confusion when it appeared to be right side up. But then they remembered to turn it upside down, and everything was fine again.

They went to the stream and placed the umbrella in the water. Then they climbed in and floated away.

"I'm floating like a coconut!" shouted Roo, jumping for joy.

Jumping for joy is a fine thing to do, but probably not when you're floating in an upside-down umbrella.

Suddenly the umbrella was right side up, and Roo and Piglet were in the water.

When they had made it safely to the bank, Roo turned to his friend.

"Thank you for helping, Piglet. But maybe floating isn't the best way to travel."

Roo went squishing off into the forest, and soon he came to the place where Eeyore lived. He found the old gray donkey eating a lunch of thistles.

"Eeyore," said Roo, "did you ever notice how cockleburs stick to your fur and get a ride?"

"How like them," said Eeyore in a low, sad voice.

Eeyore went back to munching thistles. When he wasn't looking, Roo sneaked around behind him and climbed up on his back. Eeyore looked up a moment later, but Roo appeared to be gone.

"He left," said Eeyore glumly. "But then, they all do."
He finished his lunch and moved slowly off through the
forest. So did Roo.

Roo tried to be very quiet, but he was too excited.
"I'm riding like a cocklebur!" he whispered happily.

Eeyore stopped and said, "For a moment there, I thought I heard Roo. Oh, well. I suppose my hearing isn't what it used to be."

Once again he plodded off through the forest.

Roo was happy, but he was also very tired. He held on to Eeyore for as long as he could. At last he let go and dropped to the ground.

"Hello, Roo," said Eeyore. "I was just thinking about you."

Roo yawned. He started thinking of a warm, snuggly place that was good for traveling. A place that was also good for afternoon naps.

"Thank you, Eeyore," he said, getting to his feet. "You helped me most of all."

"I did?" asked Eeyore. "Imagine that."

Roo hopped back to Kanga as fast as he could. She kissed him and helped him into her pouch. Then she gave him a pat and bounded off.

Inside, Roo smiled sleepily. He wasn't a dandelion, or a coconut, or a cocklebur. His friends had helped him to find that out. But he was Roo, with lots to see from his mama's pouch, and lots of room to grow.